To Charlie...
and his fantastic hair!

ABOUT THIS BOOK

I usually work with watercolor, gouache, and pencil. But Birdie was pleading with those big, eager eyes for something more, so I turned to collage. I collect and am always in search of interesting papers and fabrics and have piles of magazine tears with any photos of textures that catch my eye. For each illustration, I think about what will be painted and then lay out swatches of the papers and fabrics that I feel will work well together. Sometimes it comes quickly, sometimes it takes hours for me to find just the right balance of paper or fabric to use, but once I get it, I reach for my seriously sharp X-ACTO blade and cut out the shapes to glue onto the final painted piece.

Hope you enjoy! xo,

Sujean

This book was edited by Liza Baker and designed by Liz Casal under the art direction of Patti Ann Harris. The production was supervised by Jonathan Lopes, and the production editor was Wendy Dopkin.

• Little, Brown and Company • Hachette Book Group • 237 Park Avenue, New York, NY 10017 • Visit our website at www.lb-kids.com • Little, Brown and Company is a division of Hachette Book Group, Inc. • The Little, Brown name and logo are trademarks of Hachette Book Group, Inc. • The publisher is not responsible for websites (or their content) that are not owned by the publisher. • First Edition: February 2014 • Library of Congress Cataloging-in-Publication Data • Rim, Sujean. • Birdie's big-girl hair / Sujean Rim. — 1st ed. • p. cm. • Summary: When five-year-old Birdie's mother promises to take her to a salon to tame her long, unruly hair, Birdie looks at magazines and consults her friends to find the style that is perfect for her. • ISBN 978-0-316-22791-9 • [1. Hairstyles—Fiction. 2. Individuality—Fiction. 3. Mothers and daughters—Fiction.] I. Title. • PZ7.R4575Bim 2013 • [E]—dc23 • 2012039921 • 10 9 8 7 6 5 4 3 2 1 • SC • Printed in China

BIRDIE'S BIG-GIRL HAIR

SUJEAN RIM

Little, Brown and Company
New York Boston

Every morning when Birdie woke up,
she hugged her dog, Monster,
and then jumped out of bed.

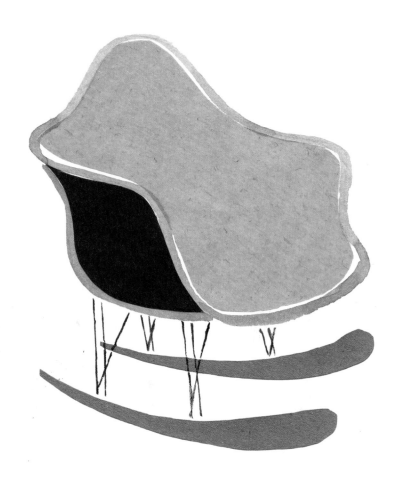

Birdie liked to start her day with some stretches.

She brushed her teeth and then her hair.

But today Birdie's hair seemed extra unruly!

It was standing up crooked where it
should have been sitting down straight.

It had tangles and fuzz balls where it
should have been silky and smooth.

Before Birdie could brush it out, she smelled something yummy coming from the kitchen.

YAY! Mommy was making breakfast!

"Good morning, Mommy!" cheered Birdie.
"Oooh! Strawberry pancakes—
my favorite!"

"Oh, sweetheart," Mommy gasped.
"Your hair has gotten so long,
I think it might be time for us
to go to the hair salon."

WOODSON

Birdie clapped with delight and pictured herself
with a big-girl hairdo.

"Mommy?" she asked. "Can I look for some
new hairstyle ideas?"

Mommy smiled at Birdie's eager face. "Absolutely.
And if you find a picture of something that's just
right, we'll bring it with us to the salon."

After breakfast, Birdie dashed off to start looking for her perfect new hairdo. She pored over Mommy's books and magazines.

"Wow, Monster! There are so many styles to choose from!"

She imagined herself with
each glamorous hairstyle:

chic, classic chignons . . .

flowing, feathery flips . . .

a bold, blunt **bob**…with bangs!

Later that day, Birdie went to the park to play with her best friends. They had some new hairdo ideas.

"How about a *bun*, like a *ballerina*!" said Coco.

"What about *spikes*, like a *rock star*!" suggested Eve.

"Or *braids*, like a *galactic princess*!" said Charlie.

But Birdie still couldn't decide.

Back home, Birdie worried she'd never find the right hairdo.
Then suddenly she discovered a book she'd never seen
before . . . Mommy's high school yearbook!

"Ooh, Monster. Look at Mommy and her gorgeous hair!"

Birdie had finally found the hairstyle of her dreams
and was ready to go to the salon.

Good Luck in College

Keep in touch!
289-6012

P.S. You're cute.

Gardner Selleck

STAY COOL, DON'T DO ANYTHING I WOULDN'T.

-MIKE

Mike Seagull

I'm going to miss you. Thanx for being a good BFF. ☺

Sofia Boogati

SMILE!

Cuz you're so awesome.

K.I.T.
861-3390

Summer Somers

Bye! Have a nice life, Billy

Billy Bjorkenson

Good luck, Martin

Martin Kickstep

I can't believe we are going to college! WOW! Stay in touch Forever! ♡ K.

Kelly LeBreck

Robin B

I'll miss you! Pat

Pat Sweeney

89

Birdie felt so special.

She put on a silky robe
and got shampooed,
conditioned, combed,
and trimmed.
Then she was brushed,
blown out, and curled.

When her hairdo was finally finished, she looked in the mirror and—

oh my!

Birdie felt so *luxurious*...

she felt so *shiny*...

she felt so . . .

full of *bounce*!

Birdie couldn't wait to go back to the park
and show her friends her new hairdo.

"Wow! Birdie, your hair looks fantastic!"

Birdie was so happy she
flew sky-high on the swings,

ran super fast playing tag,

and seesawed
like never before!

She was having such a good time that she didn't realize her new hairdo had lost its coif.

Oh no!